# RUPERT
## and the
# BIT OF MAGIC

CARNIVAL

It is the last day of term and Rupert is taking home his school report. Tigerlily, the little Chinese girl, is walking with him. She has her report too.

'I think I have good report here,' says Tigerlily happily, tapping the sealed envelope.

'I wish I could say the same,' sighs Rupert.

'I worked as hard as I could but everything seemed to go wrong this term,' he tells her. 'I'm sure my report will be one of the worst I've ever had. I hope Mum and Dad won't be too upset.'

Tigerlily looks sympathetic. 'I know what is like to have bad report,' she says. 'My daddy get very cross with me.'

Rupert chuckles. 'I'm surprised he didn't use a bit of magic to make your report better,' he jokes.

Tigerlily's daddy, of course, is the Chinese Magician – and he can do lots of things by magic.

Tigerlily claps her hands. 'That
very good idea,' she cries.

'I never think of that!'

Her eyes light up. 'I ask him to do
that for you now, yes?'

The idea makes Rupert burst out
laughing.

Tigerlily frowns at him. 'What so funny?' she asks. 'You think he not able to do easy thing like that? My daddy very very clever. He best magician in world.'

'I know that,' says Rupert quickly. 'I didn't mean it that way. I was laughing because it's a funny thing to ask him to do.'

'You think so?' She snatches the report from Rupert's hand. 'Well, we see. He coming along now.'

'Hey, wait a minute,' protests Rupert, but Tigerlily is already racing off to meet her daddy.

When Rupert catches up, the Chinese Magician gives him a strange look. 'I hear is bad report,' he says, patting the envelope. 'Is true you want me make it better?'

'Well, er – not exactly,' stutters
Rupert.

'Yes, is true,' insists Tigerlily. 'He
tells me use bit of magic to get
good report.'

'It was just a joke,' gasps Rupert.

The Chinese Magician snaps his
fingers. 'I prepare special school
report spell for you,' he says.
'Follow me.'

'Oh, crumbs!' gulps Rupert.

When they reach the Pagoda, the
amazing house where Tigerlily
and her daddy live, the Chinese
Magician looks up his Spell Book.

'Yes, is here,' he announces. 'But also is small problem.'

He peers closely at the page. 'It seems spell can go either way – maybe make better, maybe make worse. You take chance?'

'Yes, take chance,' shouts
Tigerlily.

'No, really, I don't think –' begins
Rupert, but he is too late.

The Chinese Magician has already started – and Rupert watches horrified as he places the school report in a large round bowl and sets fire to it!

Then the Magician claps a lid on
the bowl, mutters some strange
words, and turns round three
times. 'Now we see,' he murmurs.

He snatches the lid off the bowl –
and Rupert blinks in
astonishment. All trace of the fire
has disappeared and the envelope
looks just as it did, except that it
is now unsealed.

'We read what your new report
say,' exclaims the Magician,
pulling out the paper from inside.

'This bear is thoroughly lazy and
has done no work at all this term,'
he reads.

'Oh no!' cries Rupert.

'His writing is terrible, his
reading is worse, and all his sums
have the wrong answers,'
continues the Magician.

Rupert holds his head in despair.
'The spell has turned out the
wrong way,' he groans.
'Whatever shall I do?'

'Is all my fault,' wails Tigerlily. 'You not want change report in first place. Me make you do this.'

'Naughty daughter speak truth,' says the Chinese Magician sternly. 'I hope she learn good lesson from this and never want to cheat again.'

He drops the report and envelope
in the bowl, and puts the lid back
on. 'Spell not yet cold,' he
declares. 'You want me try turn
back as was?'

'Oh yes, please,' begs Rupert.

'Make no promise,' says the Magician. 'Maybe impossible now.'

But when he lifts the lid off, Rupert sees his sealed envelope back in there.

He picks it up gratefully. 'I never want to go through that again,' he breathes.

'Is lesson for you too then,' suggests the Magician softly, with a twinkle in his eye.

And later, when Rupert hands the report to his Mum and Dad, guess what?

It turns out to be not so bad after all! Lucky Rupert!

Carnival
An imprint of the Children's Division
of the Collins Publishing Group
8 Grafton Street, London W1X 3LA

First published by Dragon Books 1986
Published by Carnival 1988

Written by Len Collis
Illustrated by Jon Davis
Designed by Ralph Semmence
Copyright © The Nutwood Press Ltd 1986
Copyright © Title and character of Rupert Bear,
Express Newspapers plc 1986

ISBN 0 00 1944 60 6

Printed & bound in Great Britain by
PURNELL BOOK PRODUCTION LIMITED
A MEMBER OF BPCC plc